A BOOK OF COLORS

AND NUMBERS

Sammy Spider shivered in his web high up on the Shapiros' living room ceiling.

SAMMY SPIDER'S FIRST HANUKKAH

SYLVIA A. ROUSS

illustrated by
KATHERINE JANUS KAHN

KAR-BEN
PUBLISHING

To all the children
I have taught.
—S.R.

For my mother,
Edmina Benish Janus
who makes every day a holiday.
—K.J.K.

KAR-BEN PUBLISHING
A division of Lerner Publishing Group, Inc.
241 First Avenue North
Minneapolis, MN 55401 U.S.A.
1-800-4KARBEN

Website address: www.karben.com

Library of Congress Cataloging-in-Publication Data

Rouss, Sylvia A.
    Sammy Spider's first Hanukkah / Sylvia A. Rouss; illustrated by Katherine Janus Kahn
        p.   cm.
    Summary: After having watched the Shapiro family celebrate the different nights of Hanukkah, Sammy Spider finds that in the end he gets to share the holiday with them.
    ISBN-13: 978-0-929371-46-7 (pbk. : alk. paper)
    ISBN-10: 0-929371-46-1 (pbk. : alk. paper)
    ISBN: 978-0-7613-8935-4 (eBook)
    [1. Hanukkah—Fiction. 2. Jews—Fiction. 3. Spiders—Fiction.] I. Kahn, Katherine.
PZ7.R7622Sam 1993
[E]—dc20   92-39639

Manufactured in the United States of America
16 – BP – 2/1/13

"Look, Mother," he called. "What is Mrs. Shapiro lighting?"

"That's a menorah," answered Mrs. Spider. "The Shapiros are celebrating Hanukkah. They will light one more candle every night for eight nights."

"It's beautiful," said Sammy, as he lowered himself on a strand of webbing to take a closer look.

"Be careful!" warned Mrs. Spider. "Don't get too close."

IT WAS THE FIRST NIGHT OF HANUKKAH. Sammy stopped right above the shamash, the helper candle that Mrs. Shapiro had used to light the first candle. "Mother, the flame feels so good on my cold feet," Sammy said.

Mr. Shapiro reached into his pocket and handed Josh a bright blue dreidel.

Sammy hovered above the flame and
listened as Mrs. Shapiro told Josh the
story of the Maccabees and the miracle
of the oil. The smell of frying potato
latkes
filled
the
room.

Josh gave the dreidel a spin and squealed with delight. It was spinning   so fast that Sammy felt a little dizzy watching from above.

When the candles had melted and the flames flickered out, the Shapiros announced bedtime and took Josh upstairs.

"It's your bedtime too, Sammy," called Mrs. Spider.

Sammy climbed the strand of silk webbing and crawled into a cozy corner.

Mrs. Spider gently tucked him in.

"Mother," asked Sammy, "do you think I could have a blue dreidel to spin?"

"Silly little Sammy," his mother laughed. "Spiders don't spin dreidels. Spiders spin webs."

ON THE SECOND NIGHT OF HANUKKAH, Sammy watched expectantly as Mrs. Shapiro helped Josh light two candles. His feet were cold and he wanted to warm them near the flame again.

Tonight Mr. Shapiro gave Josh a bright red dreidel. Now he had two to spin.

Everyone sang Hanukkah songs and ate donuts filled with sweet, red cherry filling.

The spinning dreidels made Sammy even dizzier.

That night, when Mrs. Spider tucked Sammy into his soft web, he asked, "Mother, do you think I could have a red dreidel to spin?" "Silly little Sammy," his mother answered. "Spiders don't spin dreidels. Spiders spin webs."

ON THE THIRD NIGHT, Sammy
once again warmed his feet above the
menorah, and watched as the Shapiros
used the shamash to light three
candles.

They gave Josh a yellow dreidel.
Now he had three dreidels to spin.

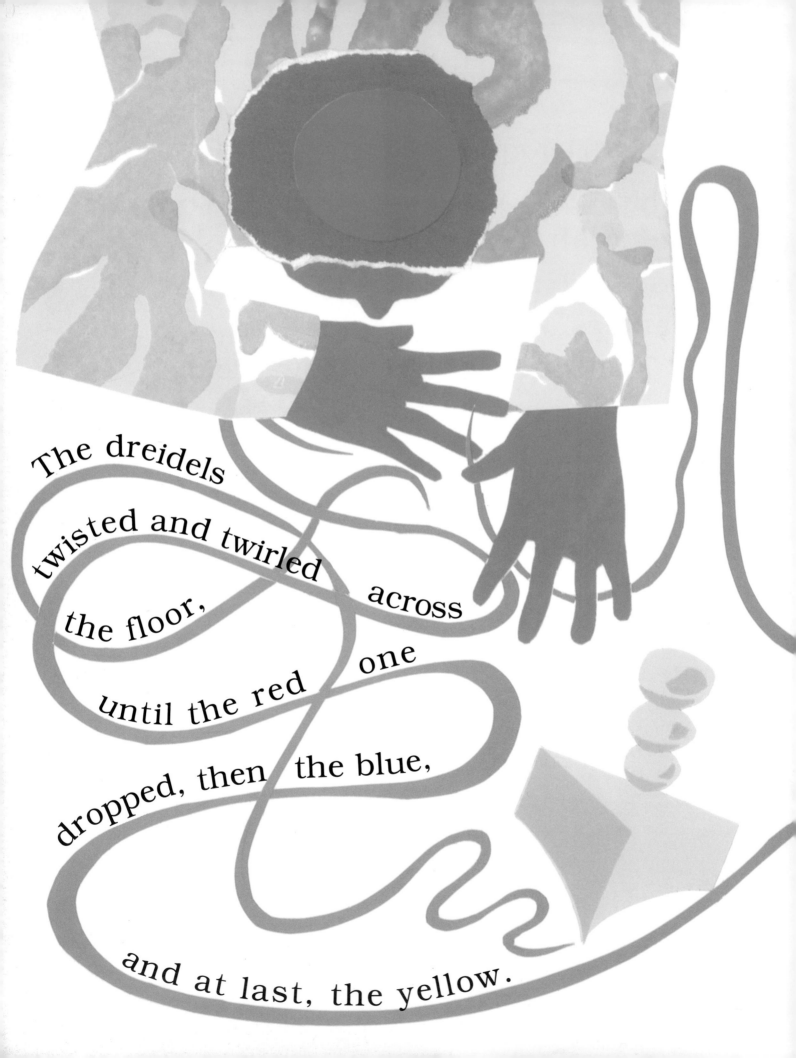

The dreidels twisted and twirled across the floor, until the red one dropped, then the blue, and at last, the yellow.

"Mother, could I have a yellow dreidel to spin?" Sammy asked at bedtime. "Silly little Sammy," she said.

"Spiders don't spin dreidels. Spiders spin webs."

Each night Sammy watched from his warm perch above the shamash.

ON THE FOURTH NIGHT, the Shapiros lit four candles and gave Josh a green dreidel.

ON THE FIFTH NIGHT, they lit five
candles and gave Josh a purple dreidel.

ON THE SIXTH NIGHT, they lit six
candles and gave Josh an orange dreidel.

ON THE SEVENTH NIGHT, they lit seven candles and Josh got a rose-colored dreidel. Sammy had to raise himself a little higher on his web because his feet were getting hot.

ON THE EIGHTH NIGHT, Sammy felt sad as he watched the Shapiros light all eight candles and give Josh a brown wooden dreidel.

"I'm going to miss Hanukkah," he thought. "I won't smell the delicious latkes. I won't hear any Hanukkah songs, I won't be able to watch Josh spin all his colorful dreidels . . . and how will I warm my feet?"

"If only I could have just one dreidel," he thought, as the eight dreidels danced merrily across the floor. "What fun I would have." Then he remembered his mother's words. "Spiders don't spin dreidels, Sammy. Spiders spin webs."

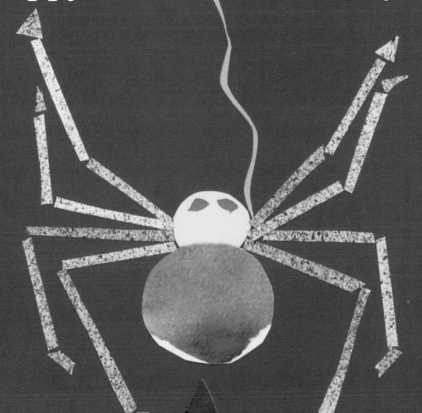

But when the last candle flickered
out and Sammy climbed reluctantly
up the web to bed, his mother smiled,
handed him a gift, and said,
    "Happy Hanukkah, Sammy."

Sammy opened the package and found eight little socks — one for each night of Hanukkah and one for each of his eight little feet. Each sock was a different color and on each one, Mrs. Spider had spun a little dreidel.

Sammy pulled on his new socks. There was

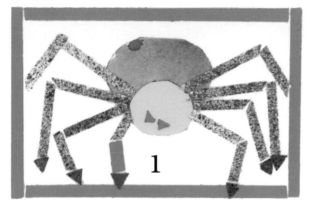

a blue one,

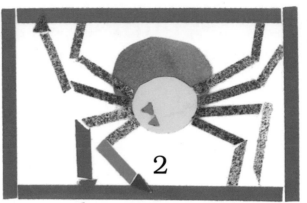

a red one,

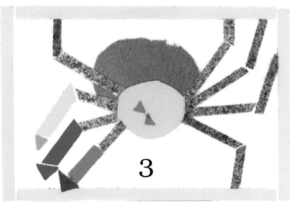

a yellow one,

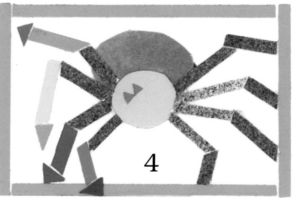

a green one,

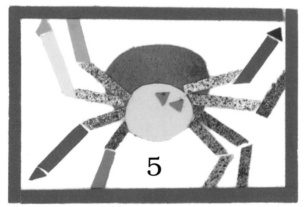

a purple one,

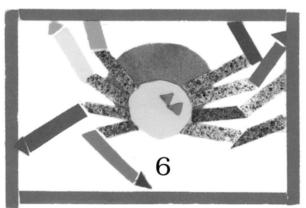

an orange one,

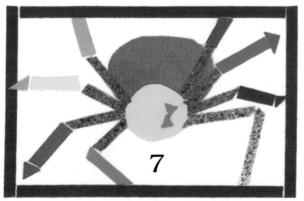

a rose-colored one,

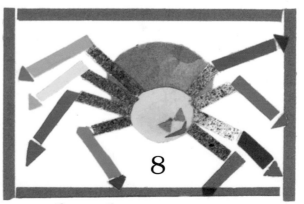

and a brown one.

He slid happily down a silky strand
and began to spin

faster

and

faster.

"Look, mother,"
he shouted.

"I'm spinning my dreidels — all eight of them!"

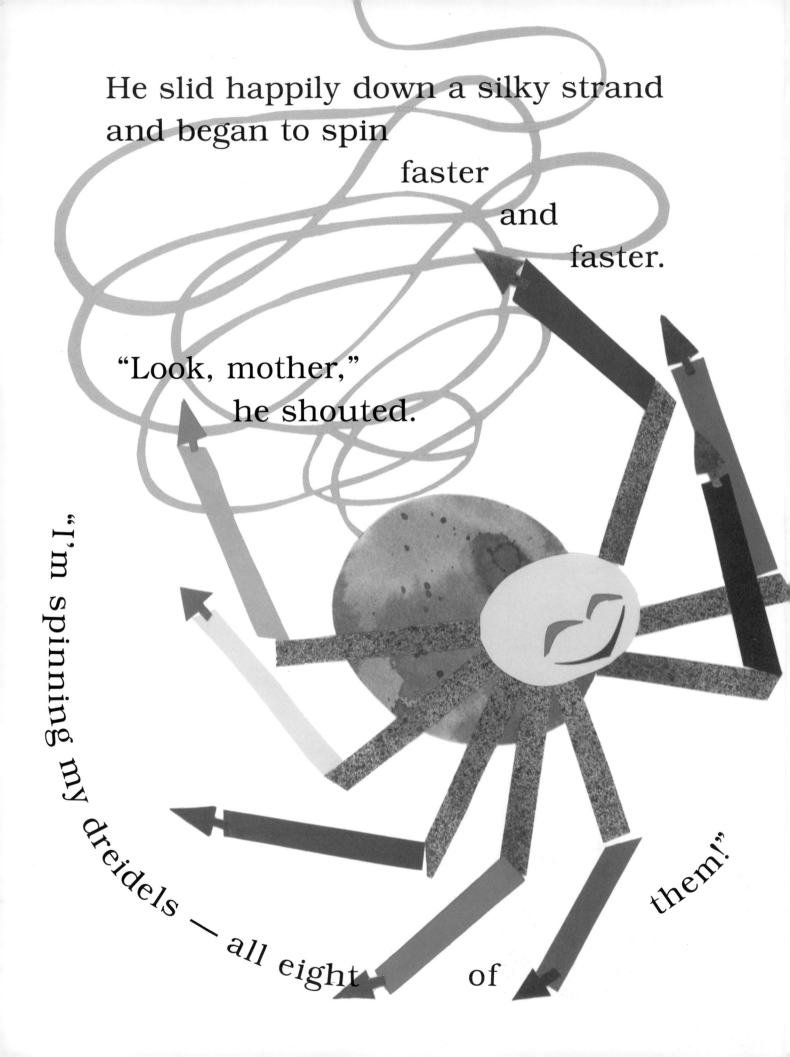